MATILDA
THE MOOCHER

story and pictures by
DIANA CAIN BLUTHENTHAL

ORCHARD BOOKS
NEW YORK

Orchard Books, 95 Madison Avenue, New York, NY 10016

Manufactured in the United States of America
Printed by Barton Press, Inc.
Bound by Horowitz/Rae
Book design by Jennifer Campbell

10 9 8 7 6 5 4 3 2 1

The text of this book is set in 20 point Cochin.
The illustrations are gouache and pen-and-ink reproduced in full color.

Library of Congress Cataloging-in-Publication Data
Bluthenthal, Diana Cain.
Matilda the moocher / story and pictures by Diana Cain Bluthenthal.
p. cm.
"A Richard Jackson book" — Half t.p.
Summary: Matilda thinks nothing of dropping by her neighbor
Libby's house to ride her bike or borrow her socks, but Libby thinks
that Matilda is taking advantage of her.
ISBN 0-531-30003-X. — ISBN 0-531-33003-6 (lib. bdg.)
[1. Borrowing and lending — Fiction.   2. Neighbors — Fiction.
3. Friendship — Fiction.   4. Schools — Fiction.]   I. Title.
PZ7.B62726Mat   1997   [E] — dc20   96-42288

This book is lovingly dedicated to
Dawn Cain
Dorothy Cain
Rosalee Sawyer
Carolyn Hampton
Buttons Walker
Dorita Beck
Renee Wayt
Rose Gustafson
Sheri Brownrigg
Kathleen Kane
Colleen Miles
Claire Frith
Trish Loar
and
in memory of
Suzi Bluthenthal

who have demonstrated to me again and again
the truth of friendship and giving.

Matilda is my next-door neighbor.
She likes to come over and ride my bike.

She also likes to stop by  when I'm having a picnic, because she loves little sandwiches.

We share my supplies in school,

and at lunch I lend her a quarter
for ice cream . . . every day.

One day, I can't find
my favorite socks.

Matilda is wearing them. I'm beginning
to think Matilda is a *moocher*.

In school I start hiding my supplies.
When Matilda asks for glue, I say I ran out.

When she comes over to ride my bike,
I say it has a flat tire.

I start having  my picnics indoors,

and I stop bringing ice cream
money to lunch.

I try to avoid Matilda as much as possible.

One day Ms. Peach makes Matilda my partner
for a class project. I start feeling sick.

I get excused to the nurse's office to lie down.
Someone else gets to be Matilda's partner.

The nurse looks at me.

"What seems to be the matter, dear?" she asks.
"I don't feel well!" I answer.

She calls my mother to come and pick me up.

All afternoon I lie in bed and think over what to do
about Matilda the Moocher. I feel worse.

My mother knocks at my door.

"Libby, you have a visitor," she tells me. "It's Matilda."

Oh *NO!* What if she wants to
RIDE MY BIKE?

What if she wants to
RIDE MY BIKE —

USE MY ART SUPPLIES —

WEAR MY
FAVORITE SOCKS —

AND STAY FOR DINNER!

In walks Matilda.

"Tell her I'm asleep!" I beg my mother.
"I think you'll feel better with some company," she says.

"Hello, Libby," Matilda starts. "I want to . . ."
OH NO! HERE IT COMES!

"I want to give you this get-well card I made
for you in class — everybody signed it," she says.
"And these cupcakes . . . we could have a picnic
in here today."

I rub my eyes. Is this *MATILDA?* Yes, it's her.
She's wearing my hat.

Matilda tells me about the class project and who she had to be partners with — *HAROLD EUGENE*.

He glued her notebook together and put crayons in his nose and chewed up her eraser.

She says she desperately hopes I feel better soon. . . .

And I do feel better, thanks to Matilda.